Duke

Saddle Up Series
Book 23

D0730282

    Dave and Pat Sargent are longtime residents of Prairie Grove, Arkansas. Dave, a fourth-generation dairy farmer, began writing in early December 1990. Pat, a former teacher, began writing shortly after. They enjoy the outdoors and have a real love for animals.

Duke

Saddle Up Series
Book 23

By Dave and Pat Sargent

Beyond "The End"
By Sue Rogers

Illustrated by Jane Lenoir

Ozark Publishing, Inc.
P.O. Box 228
Prairie Grove, AR 72753

Cataloging-in-Publication Data

Sargent, Dave, 1941—
    Duke / by Dave and Pat Sargent ; illustrated
by Jane Lenoir.—Prairie Grove, AR : Ozark
Publishing, c2004.
        p. cm. (Saddle up series ; 23)
        "Good behavior"—Cover.
        SUMMARY: Roger Sherman's dappled
palomino horse witnesses the meeting at which
it is decided to break away from British rule
and later, the signing of the Declaration of
Independence. Includes factual information
about dappled palomino horses.
        ISBN 1-56763-681-0 (hc)
                1-56763-682-9 (pbk)
        1. Horses—Juvenile fiction. 2. Sherman,
Roger, 1721–1793—Juvenile fiction. 3. United
States. Declaration of Independence—Juvenile
fiction. [1. Sherman, Roger, 1721–1793—Fiction.
2. United States. Declaration of Independence—
Fiction. 3. Palomino horse—Fiction. 4. Horses—
Fiction. 5. United States—Politics and
government—1783-1809—Fiction.]
I. Sargent, Pat, 1936– II. Lenoir, Jane, 1950– ill.
III. Title. IV. Series.
        PZ7.S2465Du 2004
        [Fic]—dc21   2001003082

iv

Inspired by

the pretty palominos Pat's uncle raised on a beautiful ranch in Texas. Some were dappled.

Dedicated to

all kids who love beautiful golden and dappled palomino horses.

Foreword

Duke the dappled palomino is there when the colonies decide to break away from British rule. Duke's boss, Roger Sherman, makes history July 4, 1776, when he signs the Declaration of Independence with Thomas Jefferson and John Adams.

Contents

If you would like to have the authors of the Saddle Up Series visit your school, free of charge, call 1-800-321-5671 or 1-800-960-3876.

One

The Lightning Bolt

Voices from within the building echoed through the quiet of late evening. Duke peeked around the doorway and looked at the group of men who were seated at a long table. "Hmmm," he thought, "this meeting may get interesting. I wonder how Boss feels about America breaking away from British rule?" Suddenly he saw his boss, Roger Sherman, stand up.

"I think," the dappled palomino said, "that I'm about to find out."

The other men at the table became silent as the most famous citizen of the colonies cleared his throat to speak.

"You men know that I don't like violent and radical behavior," Roger said.

"Right on, Boss! Neither do I," the dappled palomino neighed.

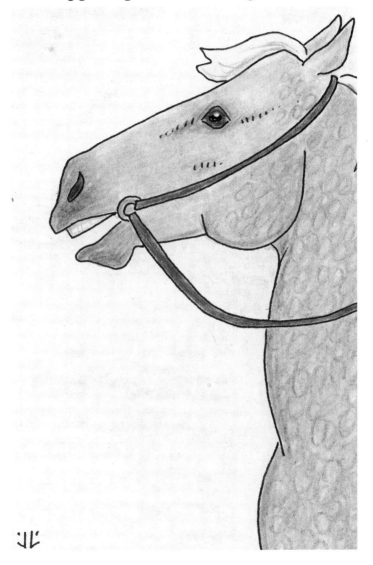

"But," Roger continued in a forceful voice, "I also know that our American colonies must become independent from Great Britain's rule. We should be in control of our own laws and regulations."

When murmurs of agreement followed his comments, he sat down. Then Thomas Jefferson stood up. Duke looked at Popcorn Blue Corn, who was dozing at the hitching rail.

"Hey," Duke whispered, "don't you want to hear your boss in action, Popcorn? He's getting ready to speak."

"I'm too tired," the blue corn mumbled. "Boss and I had to run to make this meeting, and I'm pooped."

"Okay, okay," Duke said with a nod of his head. "But you're missing out on history-making news."

"That's okay by me," Popcorn muttered as he drifted off to sleep.

Duke turned his attention back to Thomas Jefferson.

"I suggest that we go ahead and appoint a council of men to compile our declaration of independence," Thomas said.

Again the men who were seated around the table agreed. Duke was tired, too. He yawned and walked over to the hitching post to wait for Roger and the other men to adjourn the meeting for the night.

An hour later, Duke smiled as he dreamed of his boss patting him gently on the shoulder. Then he realized that he was not dreaming. He blushed with embarrassment and opened one eye.

"Wake up, Duke," Roger said with a chuckle. "Surely our meeting was not that dull."

"Oops," the dappled palomino mumbled as he opened his other eye.

"Sorry, Boss. There was not one thing boring about this meeting. It was history in the making!"

Suddenly thunder rumbled in the distance. When Duke looked to the west, he saw constant flashes of lightning and a big menacing cloud. It was about the blackest cloud he had ever seen.

"Uh-oh, Boss," he groaned. "Look at that bad storm coming our way. I don't think we can beat it home. It will catch us before we get there. Let's get going."

And sure enough, thirty to forty minutes later, huge raindrops pelted the countryside as Duke loped through the night toward home.

"Hang on, Boss," he neighed loudly as he suddenly skidded to a halt at the edge of a washed-out bridge. His hooves slid on the mud and stopped dangerously close to the edge of the flooding creek.

"Duke!" Roger shouted above the sound of the rain and flooding waters. "We have to find shelter and wait for the storm to subside."

"I agree, Boss," the dappled palomino groaned quietly. "I just don't know how to keep my feet under me until we find that shelter."

He slowly and carefully backed up several feet before attempting to turn around. "Whew," he thought. "So far, so good. I think we're safe from the flooding creek waters."

The dappled palomino was just beginning to feel more confidence in his footing and himself. He was also feeling confident in his ability to take care of his very important boss when the heavens seemed to open up. The blanket of pouring rain and the soggy countryside were suddenly illuminated by a lightning bolt. It struck a tree mere feet from the two. Duke felt the impact, and then his world turned black.

Two

Duke's Young Nurse

Frogs and crickets were singing to the night when Duke awoke. He was lying on his side, and his mind was clouded with little bits and pieces of memory. "Boss and I were on our way to a meeting," he thought. "It was an important meeting. Now I remember! Boss and his colleagues are going to draw a plan for the American colonies to separate from...from...Great Britain. Oh no! The storm! Where's Boss?" He tried to stand up, but a heavy weight

was holding him down. His world
again went black.

When he opened his eyes, the sun was up. Voices were echoing amid the cheerful songs of the birds.

"You fellows hurry up and get that limb off the dappled palomino," one man yelled. "We'll take care of Mr. Sherman."

Duke saw several men walking toward him. He again tried to stand, but the heavy branch held him down. He quietly waited as they heaved and lifted the weight from his body. A moment later, he was standing, but his left hind foot throbbed with pain.

"This horse is hurt," one of the men said. "They took Mr. Sherman to some folks who live near here. Maybe those folks wouldn't mind taking care of this dappled palomino, too. That hind foot looks bad!"

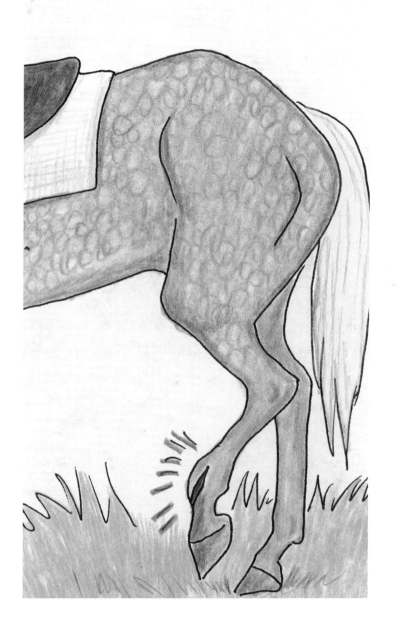

"That's the Barber family," one of the men offered. "I know them. They're good people. They'll take good care of both of them."

"Hmmm," Duke thought. "Boss is hurt. I hope he's going to be okay. Those Barber folks better be good to him."

An hour later, Duke was resting in a clean stall with fresh hay. His body ached and his foot throbbed. Suddenly he saw a small girl enter the barn. She had cute freckles across her nose and a friendly smile. Her long black hair bounced against her back as she ran to the stall.

"Hi, Duke," she said with a grin. "My name is Patricia. My folks are taking care of your owner, so I'm going to take care of you. I think we'll be real good friends."

"I think so, too," Duke nickered as he nuzzled her on the cheek. His life seemed to be improving every minute.

Patricia giggled and stroked him on his nose. Moments later, she was cleaning the wound on his hind foot with a soft cloth.

During the next two weeks, Duke and Patricia spent many hours together. With whinnies and neighs, Duke told her about his boss.

"Roger Sherman, my boss, has been a farmer, a shoemaker, owner of a general store, and a surveyor," he nickered. "Actually, he's the county surveyor, and that," Duke added proudly, "is one very lucrative position!"

With each visit, Patricia brushed Duke's golden coat. She always made it shine.

"Boss also made a series of annual almanacs," Duke continued. "And now he is a representative for New Haven in the legislature." The dappled palomino nuzzled Patricia on the hand as he added, "That means he's a politician."

Late one evening, Duke was surprised when he saw Patricia enter the barn.

"It's way past your bedtime, my little friend," he nickered softly. "Uh-oh," he groaned as he spotted tears streaming down her cheeks. "What's wrong?"

"Your owner is all healed up," she whimpered.

"Oh, Patricia," he whinnied, "that's wonderful news."

She rubbed the big tears from her eyes with one small fist before saying, "That means you have to leave tomorrow, Duke."

Duke felt that his heart would break as he listened to the little girl sob.

"I'll see you again, Patricia," he murmured softly as he nuzzled her black hair. "I promise to come back to visit you. Boss has important business to do, but when he gets through with the declaration, I'll come to see you."

Forty-five minutes later, Duke silently watched Patricia as she slept on a soft bed of hay in the stall. He heard the barn door squeak as it opened, and Mr. Barber entered. Duke whinnied softly and nodded his head toward the sleeping child.

The man gently lifted Patricia from the hay and chuckled.

"Well, Duke," he said, "you have found a lifelong friend in my little daughter. You must come back one day to visit her."

"I will," Duke murmured. "I'll come back and see Patricia every chance I get. I promise."

Three

The Fourth of July

It was summertime when Duke and his boss returned to the Barber home to thank them again for their hospitality. Several months had passed since the dappled palomino and Roger Sherman had healed and gone home. As they approached the house, Duke hit a fast trot. His ears were forward, and his eyes darted from side to side, trying to locate his little dark-headed friend.

"Whoa, Duke," Roger said with a chuckle. "That trot of yours is too rough. Slow down a bit. You'll see Patricia without using that body-pounding gait of yours."

Minutes later, a happy reunion took place between Roger Sherman and the Barber family, but Patricia was nowhere in sight.

As Duke silently lowered his head, a big tear rolled down his cheek and fell onto the ground.

Suddenly the dappled palomino heard a very familiar voice in the distance, and he raised his head high.

"Duke!" the voice squealed. "Duke, is that really you?"

The dappled palomino trotted toward the dark-headed girl running up the path toward him.

"Patricia," he nickered. "I'm so happy to see you. I promised that I would come back."

A short time later, Duke and Patricia stood and listened as Roger and Mr. Barber talked about national business.

"Duke and I," Roger said, "are on our way to the Pennsylvania State House in Philadelphia to sign the Declaration of Independence."

"I am very pleased," Mr. Barber said. "The American colonies should be free of British rule."

Patricia winked at Duke and whispered, "Father wants us to be our own boss."

"Your father is a smart fellow," Duke said with a grin. "Boss has worked hard to make this happen."

Suddenly a worried frown appeared on Roger's face.

"I am concerned," he said, "that this break from the Crown may bring a backlash of problems, and I hate violence and bad behavior."

Mr. Barber nodded his head. "You are thinking that we may have to go to war, aren't you?"

The dappled palomino gulped, and Patricia caught her breath.

"Yes," Roger agreed. "War will likely be fought with Great Britain. We must be ready to fight for our freedom."

"I will fight," Duke snorted.

"I will help," Patricia vowed.

"My family," Mr. Barber stated, "will be ready to do what is needed to help."

Three hours later, Duke and Boss Roger Sherman left the Barber home, vowing to return soon.

The mood of the horses was excited happiness as they met in

front of the Pennsylvania State House on July 4th, 1776. On that day, the Declaration of Independence was signed. Duke looked all around and saw Popcorn Blue Corn talking to a bay sabino and a chocolate chestnut.

"Hey, Popcorn!" Duke neighed loudly. "Good to see you again."

Popcorn's ears shot forward, and he quickly trotted over to Duke.

"This is a fun meeting, Duke," he said with a chuckle. "I have been visiting with the other horses, and they say their bosses have been as busy and excited as mine." The blue corn moved closer and whispered, "My boss, Thomas Jefferson, wrote the declaration they signed today."

Duke whispered, "And each man here helped with the decision."

Popcorn timidly drew a line in the dirt with one hoof as he said, "Sorry, Duke. I did not mean to brag about my boss."

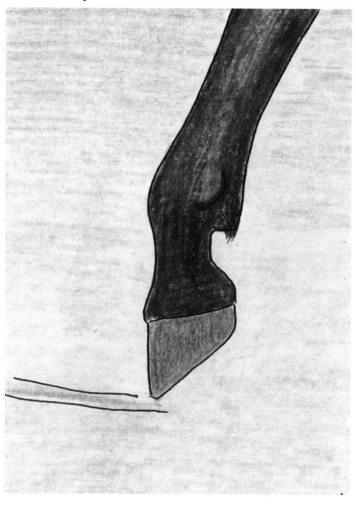

"Aw, that's okay," Duke said. "Your boss is one great American. But so is every boss here today."

"Hmmm," Duke thought as he waited for the end of the meeting. "July 4, 1776 is a day that will go down in history as one of the most important days in the colonies. I know that folks will remember Thomas Jefferson and John Adams and Roger Sherman as they see the names on this declaration."

"But," he nickered softly, "I do wonder if they will remember the dappled palomino named Duke who traveled with Roger Sherman. Aw, it's okay," he said with a chuckle. "Life is great in America!"

Four

Dappled Palomino Facts

Palominos are yellow, and sometimes gold. They have light manes and tails. Dapples are very common on palominos.

Dappling is a network of darker areas over lighter areas and can be on any color horses. Dapples can even be seen on black horses. Dappling is most noticeable when horses shed hair coats in the spring and fall. On some, like the silver dapple and grey dapple, it is visible throughout the year.

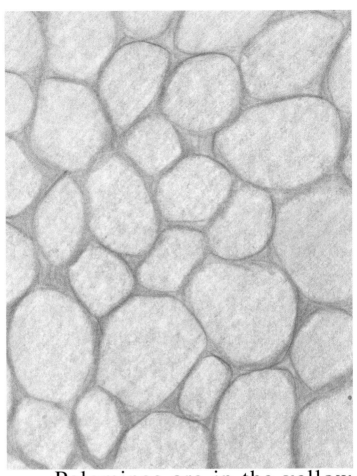

Palominos are in the yellow dun group of horses. For many years, most horse owners considered palominos a separate group from the other duns.

BEYOND "THE END"

Definition–Gallop: The customary gait a horse chooses when returning to the stable.

Anonymous

WORD LIST

dappled palomino
knee
14 hands and 2 inches
ears pointing back
forearm
popcorn blue corn
ears pointing forward
18 hands and 4 inches
bay sabino
heel
14 hands and 5 inches
chest
ears pointed up
10 hands and 6 inches

chocolate chestnut
12 hands and 2 inches
shoulder
medicine hat paint
thigh
Chincoteague
elbow
dapple gray

From the word list above, write:
1. One word that names a breed of pony.
2. Three word groups that tell the direction a pony might point his ears. Which direction shows your pony is interested, angry, or contented?
3. Five words for color names for ponies.
4. Five measurements of horse heights. Are they all the heights of ponies? Which heights are too tall to be ponies?
5. Seven words that name points on a pony that are the same as parts of a human body. Are they in the same place? Where is the forearm, heel, and elbow on a pony?

CURRICULUM CONNECTIONS

Which signer of the Declaration of Independence was a shoemaker by trade before he taught himself law?

Roger Sherman lived with his family in Newton, Massachusetts. When his father died, young Roger worked and provided for his mother and younger siblings. They later moved to be with his oldest brother who lived in New Milford, Connecticut. Roger made the trip on foot, carrying his tools on his back.

Find these two cities on a map and figure the distance between them. How far did Roger Sherman walk?

Name two of the tensions with the British that eventually led to the writing of the Declaration of Independence in 1776. For answers, go to the Library of

Congress website <www.americas library.gov/cgi-bin/page.cgi/jb/revolut>.

During this period of time in our new country, on September 26, 1775, a baby was born who would grow up and walk 100,000 square miles of Midwestern wilderness and prairie, planting apple seeds? Who was this man? See <www.americaslibrary.gov/cgi-bin/page.cgi/jb/revolut/apple_1>.

PROJECT

Combine your math and artistic skills! Draw to scale and accurately color a picture (body, tail, and mane) of the horse that is featured in each book read in the Saddle Up Series. You could soon have sixty horses prancing around the walls of your classroom!
Learning + horses = FUN.

Look in your school library media center for books about how to draw a horse and the colors of horses. Don't forget the useful information in the last chapter of this book (Dappled Palomino Facts) and the picture on the book cover for a shape and color guide.

HELPFUL HINTS AND WEBSITES
A horse is measured in hands. One hand equals four inches. Use a scale of 1" equals 1 hand.

Visit website <www.equisearch.com> to find a glossary of equine terms, information about tack and equipment, breeds, art and graphics, and more about horses. Learn more at <www.horse-country.com> and at <www.ansi.okstate.edu/breeds/horses/>.

KidsClick! is a web search for kids by librarians. There are many interesting websites here. HORSES and HORSE-MANSHIP are two of the more than 600 subjects. Visit <www.kidsclick.org>.

Is your classroom beginning to look like the Rocking S Horse Ranch? Happy Trails to You!

ANSWERS (Roger Sherman was apprenticed to a shoemaker as a very young man.)